Forest Hill Elementary School
2407 Rocks Road
Forest Hill, MD 21050

2023

FARMYARD FAIRY TALES
Rampunzel

Written by Alicia Rodriguez   Illustrated by Srimalie Bassani

A Blossoms Beginning Readers Book

CRABTREE
Publishing Company
www.crabtreebooks.com

BLOSSOMS BEGINNING READERS LEVEL GUIDE

Level 1 Early Emergent Readers Grades PK-K
Books at this level have strong picture support with carefully controlled text and repetitive patterns. They feature a limited number of words on each page and large, easy-to-read print.

Level 2 Emergent Readers Grade 1
Books at this level have a more complex sentence structure and more lines of text per page. They depend less on repetitive patterns and pictures. Familiar topics are explored, but with greater depth.

Level 3 Early Readers Grade 2
Books at this level are carefully developed to tell a great story, but in a format that children are able to read and enjoy by themselves. They feature familiar vocabulary and appealing illustrations.

Level 4 Fluent Readers Grade 3
Books at this level have more text and use challenging vocabulary. They explore less familiar topics and continue to help refine and strengthen reading skills to get ready for chapter books.

School-to-Home Support for Caregivers and Teachers

This book helps children grow by letting them practice reading. Here are a few guiding questions to help the reader with building his or her comprehension skills. Possible answers appear here in red.

Before Reading:
- What do I think this story will be about?
  - I think this story will be about about a princess.
  - I think this story will be about animals.

During Reading:
- Pause and look at the words and pictures. Why did the character do that?
  - The witch put Rampunzel in a tower so she would only sing to her.
  - Rampunzel leaves her tower because the Prince helps her run away.

After Reading:
- Describe your favorite part of the story.
  - My favorite part was when Rampunzel let down her hair.
  - My favorite part was when the Prince helped Rampunzel out of the tower.

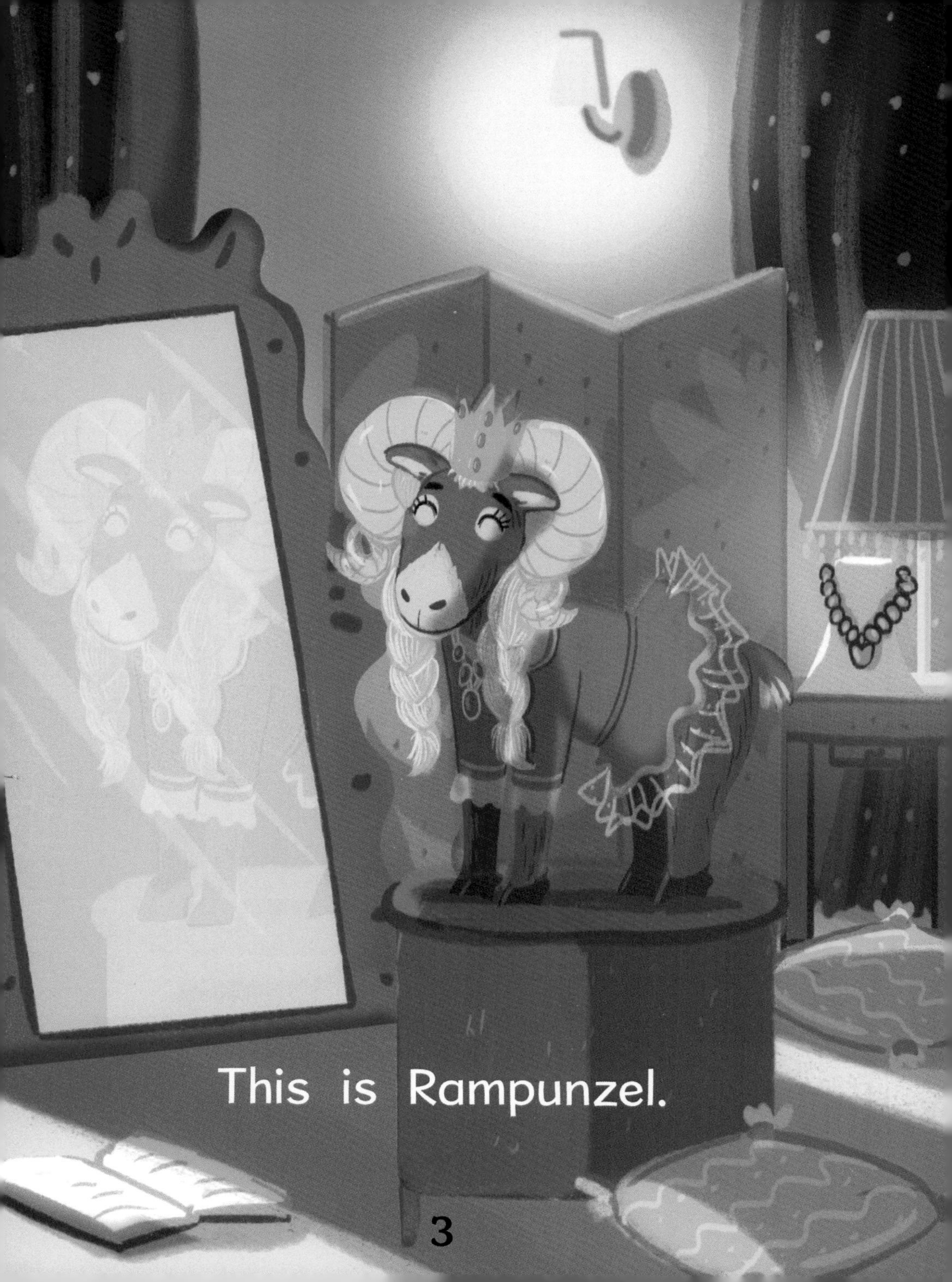

This is Rampunzel.

Rampunzel was great
at singing.

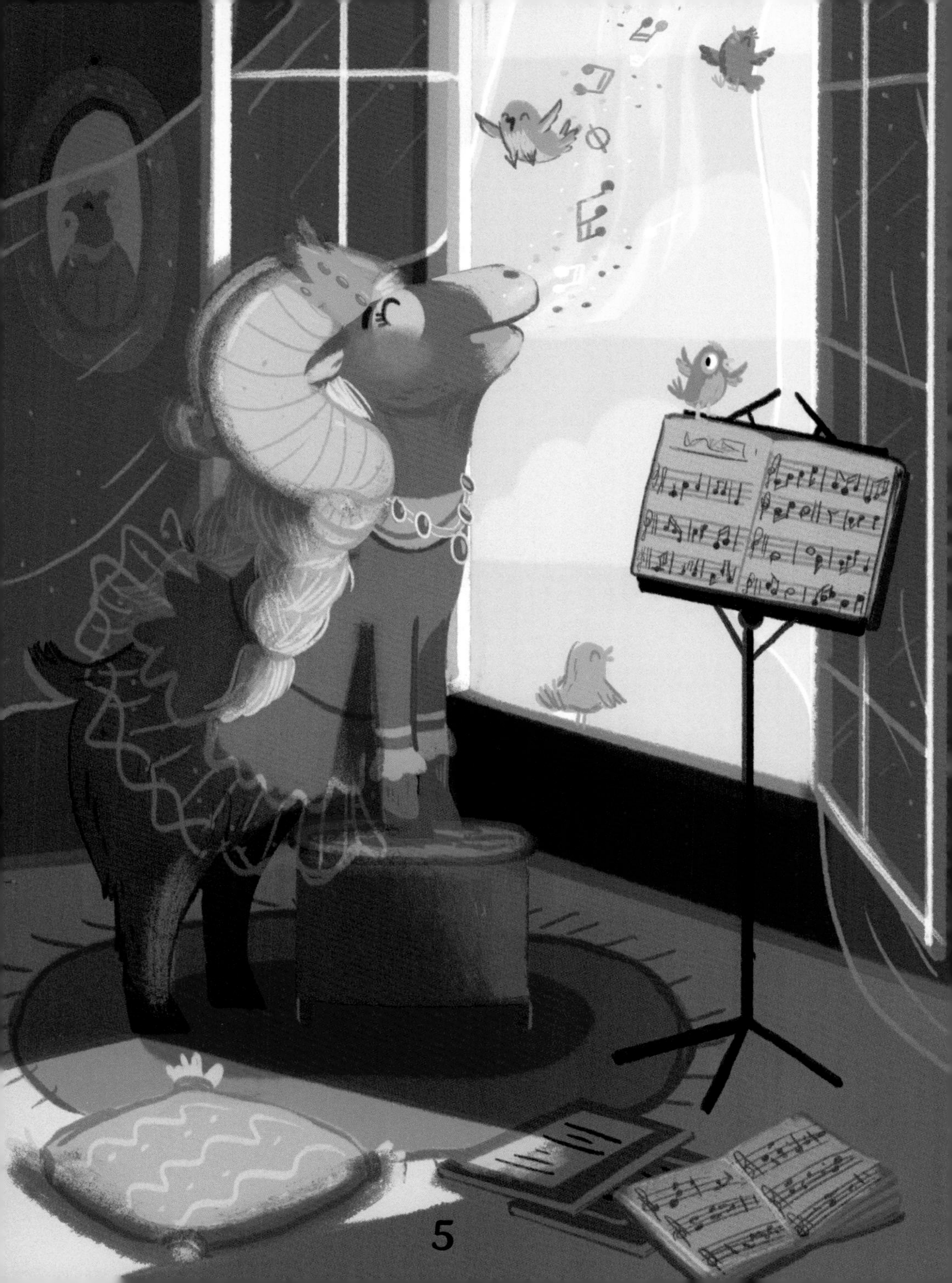

One day a witch found Rampunzel and locked her away.

She wanted Rampunzel to sing only for her.

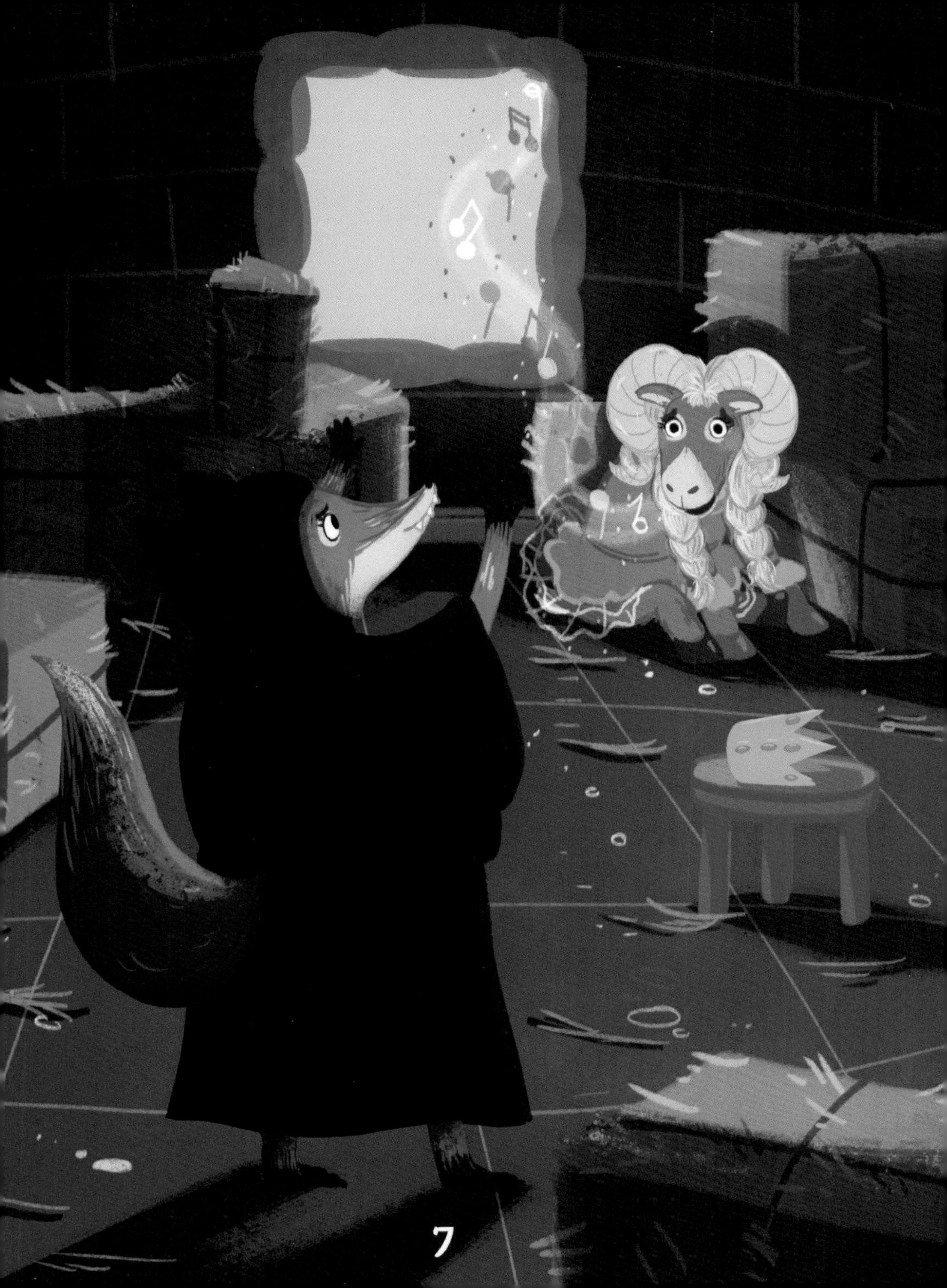

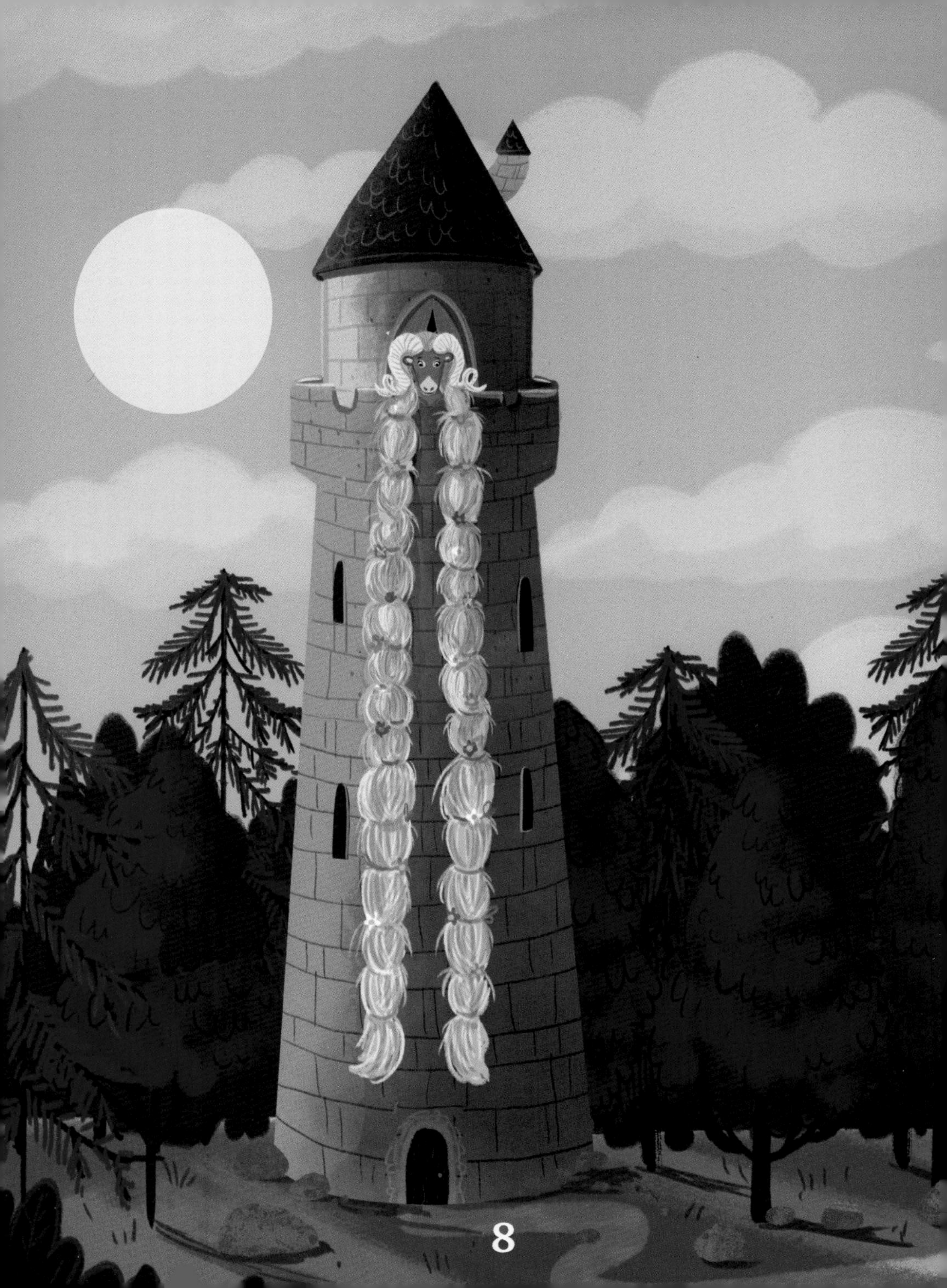

After many years, Rampunzel's hair was very long.

"Rampunzel, Rampunzel, let down your hair!"

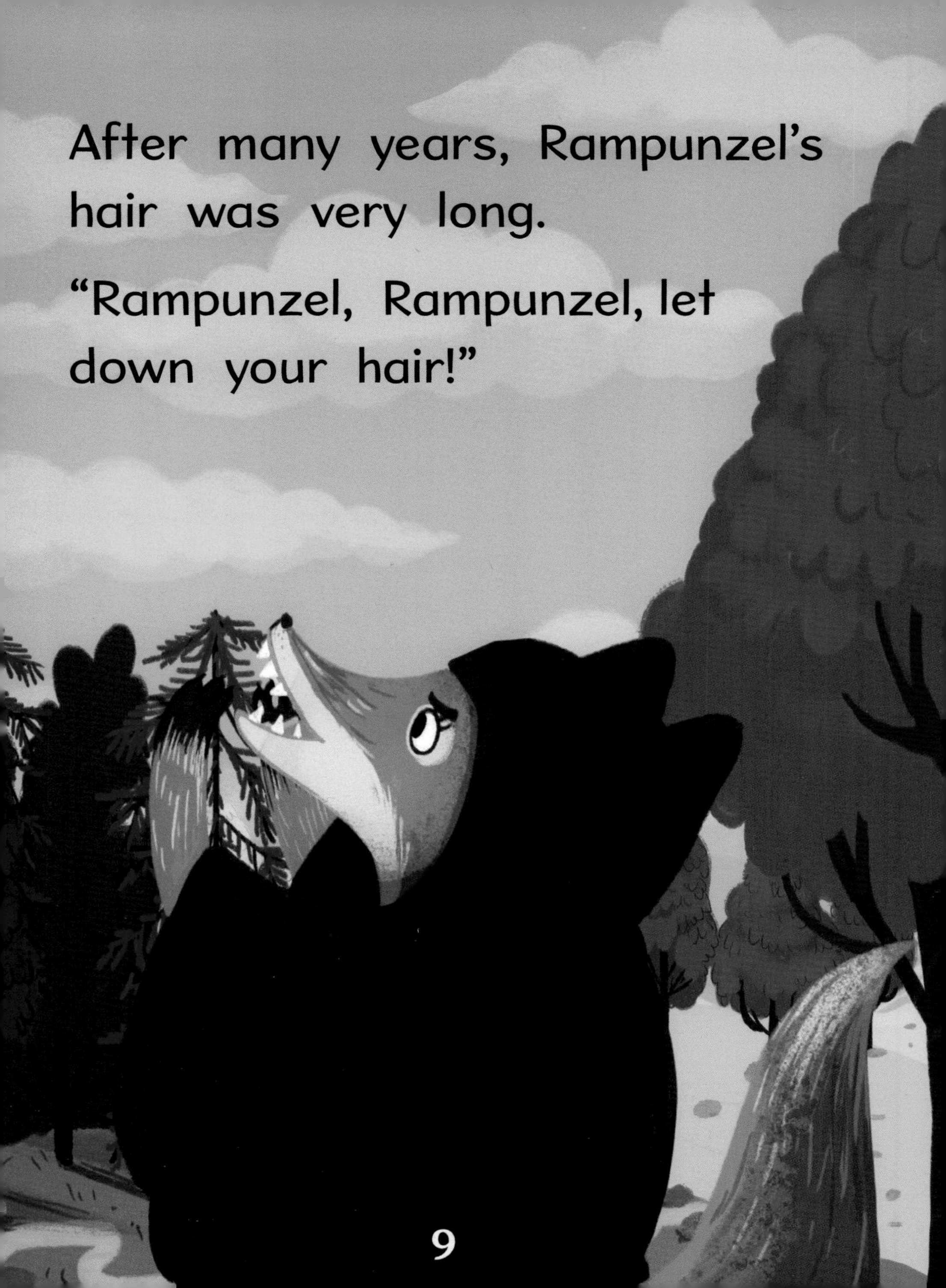

A prince finds Rampunzel!

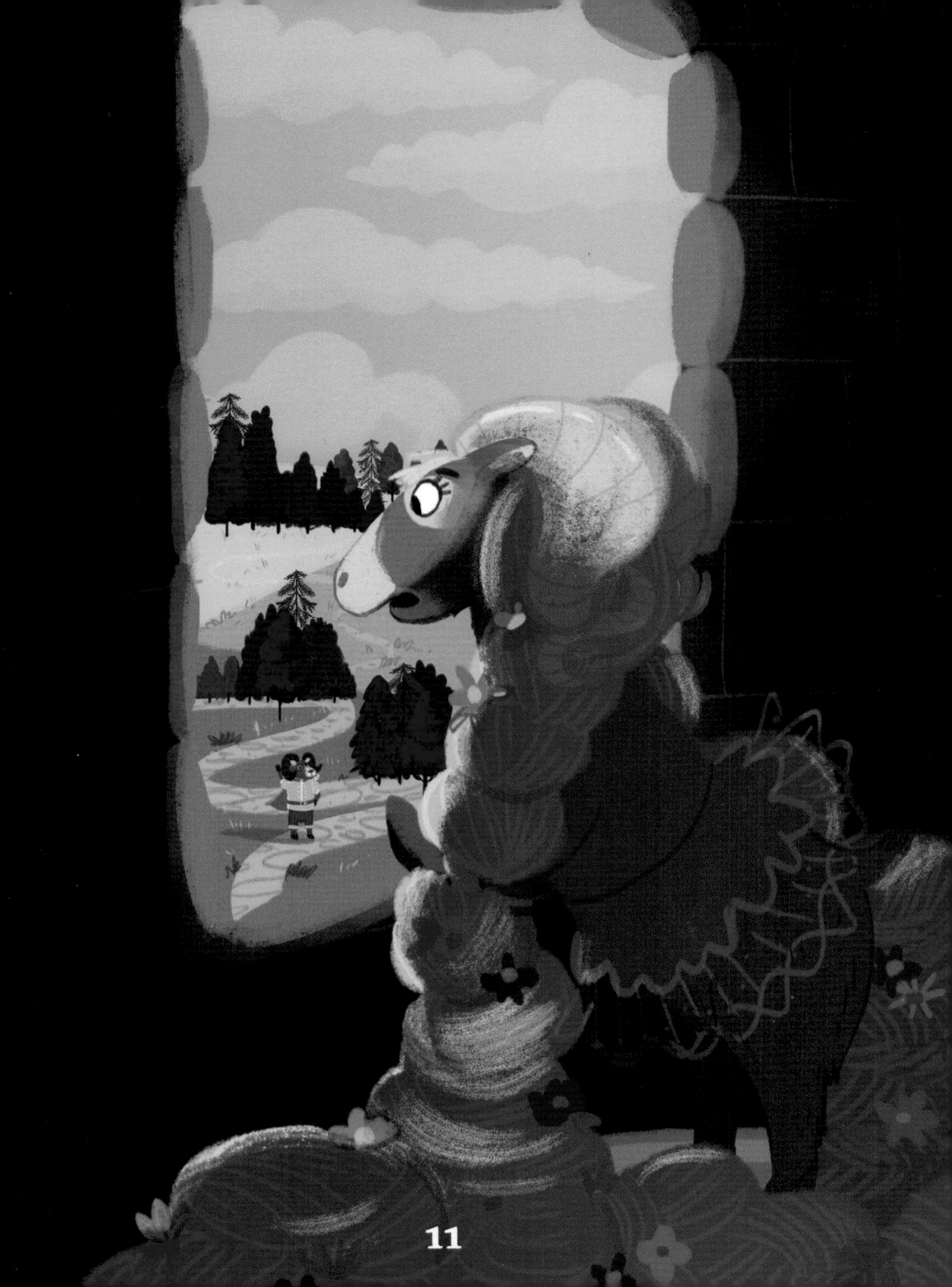

With help from the prince,
Rampunzel runs away!

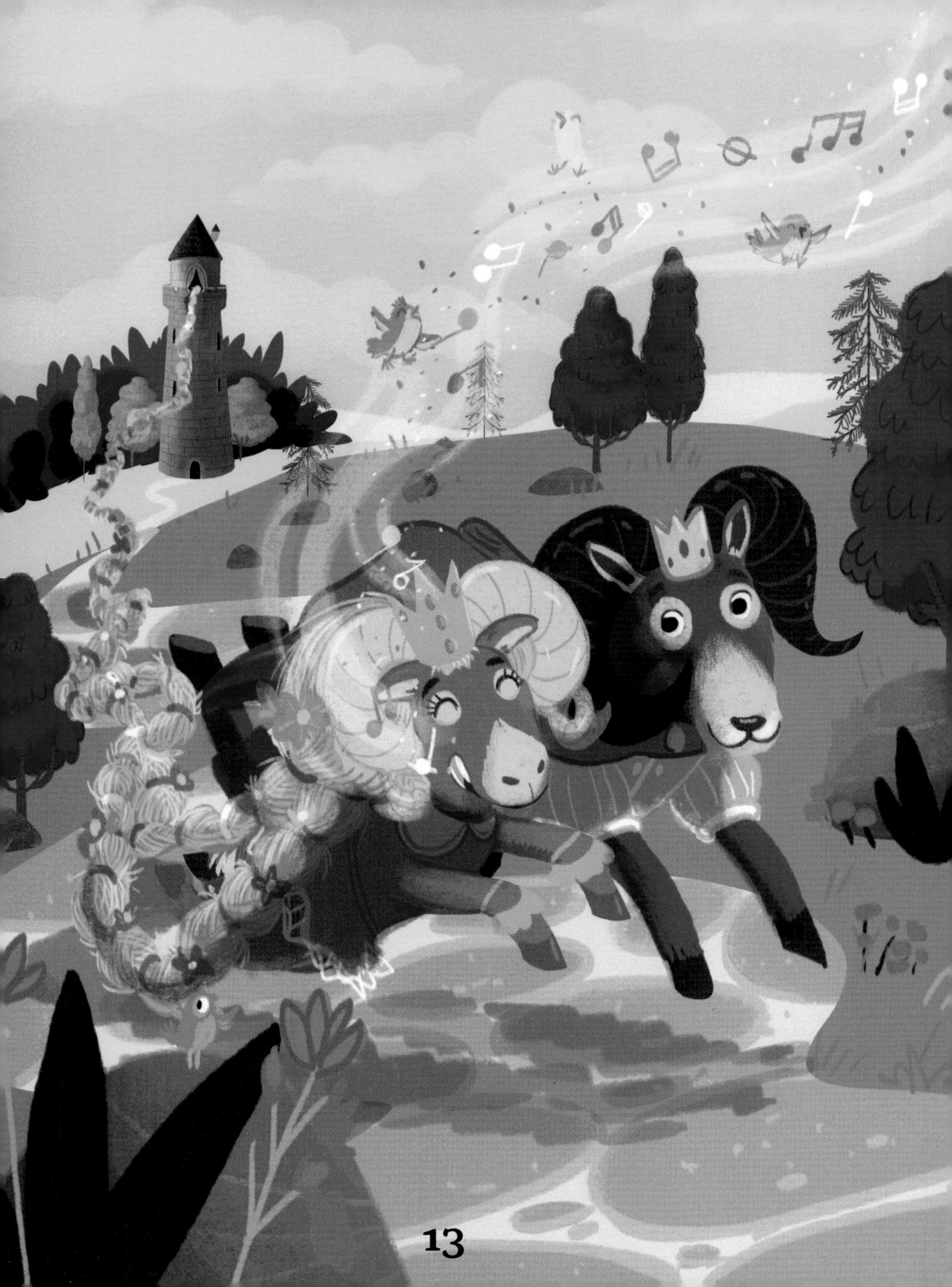

WRITING PROMPTS

Possible answers appear here in red.

1. **Write a different ending to the story.**

Rampunzel learned magic from the witch, and escaped the tower using a spell.

2. **Choose a character and write the story from that character's point of view.**

The witch was actually a good witch. She took Rampunzel to a tower in order to give her the best singing lessons in the world!

3. **Write about a similar situation that you experienced.**

At recess, my friend came to help me down from the really tall monkey bars.

ABOUT THE AUTHOR

Alicia Rodriguez has loved reading and writing fairy tales her entire life. When she isn't writing her next book, Alicia loves to play board games with friends, and travel to new and exciting places. She lives in a beautiful home by the ocean in British Columbia, Canada.

ABOUT THE ILLUSTRATOR

Srimalie Bassani was born in 1986 and lives and works in Mantova, Italy. Her mother gave her a passion for drawing and painting and always encourages her artistic expression. Srimalie attended the Academy of Fine Arts and was later selected for a Master's Degree in Illustration Editorial, "ARS in FABULA," in Macerata.

Srimalie's work is always full of surprises. She likes to diversify her style based on the story she is illustrating, and enjoys drawing in pencil, and then applying color with a graphic tablet. Since 2012, she has illustrated for various publishers.

CRABTREE
Publishing Company

FARMYARD FAIRY TALES
Rampunzel

Written by: Alicia Rodriguez
Illustrations by: Srimalie Bassani
Art direction and layout by:
Under the Oaks Media
Series Development: James Earley
Proofreader: Kathy Middleton
Educational Consultant:
Marie Lemke M.Ed.
Print and production coordinator:
Katherine Berti

Library and Archives Canada Cataloguing in Publication

Title: Rampunzel / written by Alicia Rodriguez ; illustrated by Srimalie Bassani.
Names: Rodriguez, Alicia (Children's author), author. | Bassani, Srimalie, illustrator.
Description: Series statement: Farmyard fairy tales | "A blossoms beginning readers book".
Identifiers: Canadiana (print) 20210222719 | Canadiana (ebook) 20210222727 | ISBN 9781427151629 (hardcover) | ISBN 9781427151681 (softcover) | ISBN 9781427151742 (HTML) | ISBN 9781427151803 (EPUB) | ISBN 9781427151865 (read-along ebook)
Classification: LCC PS8635.O374 R36 2022 | DDC jC813/.6—dc23

Library of Congress Cataloging-in-Publication Data

Names: Rodriguez, Alicia (Children's author), author. | Bassani, Srimalie, illustrator.
Title: Rampunzel / written by Alicia Rodriguez ; illustrated by Srimalie Bassani.
Other titles: Rapunzel. English.
Description: New York, NY : Crabtree Publishing Company, [2022] | Series: Farmyard fairy tales
Identifiers: LCCN 2021022797 (print) | LCCN 2021022798 (ebook) | ISBN 9781427151629 (hardcover) | ISBN 9781427151681 (paperback) | ISBN 9781427151742 (ebook) | ISBN 9781427151803 (epub) | ISBN 9781427151865
Subjects: LCSH: Readers (Primary) | LCGFT: Readers (Publications). | Picture books. | Adaptations.
Classification: LCC PE1119.2 .R637 2022 (print) | LCC PE1119.2 (ebook) | DDC 428.6/2--dc23
LC record available at https://lccn.loc.gov/2021022797
LC ebook record available at https://lccn.loc.gov/2021022798

Crabtree Publishing Company

Printed in Canada/052022/CPC20220502

www.crabtreebooks.com   1-800-387-7650

Published in the United States
Crabtree Publishing
347 Fifth Avenue, Suite 1402-145
New York, NY, 10016

Published in Canada
Crabtree Publishing
616 Welland Ave.
St. Catharines, ON, L2M 5V6

16